DREAMS in the NIGHT

This is a work of memories and is intended as an escapist read. Characters, settings, names, and story/scenes/occurrences may have names changed due to privacy, places or settings and/or occurrences. Any incidences of resemblance to other works are purely coincidental. This edition is published by agreement. 2020.

Share your Dream's

this may be something   someone
needs to see!

By, Jeannie Lynn.

Content is, as following.

1 Growing Up with Listing to Lore Lyn 's,

2 Dream is of a house

 3 THE HAPPY PLACE,

4 Wealthy Cowboy

 5 Lost and Not Knowing Who I am.

 6 Dreamers Paradise

 7 Farid of the Unknown,

8 Wolves & Coyotes with Wild Cats,

9 Dream of a Flea Market

10 The Wish Class,

 11 The Apartment Complex

1. Dreams in the Night's by,

Jeannie Lynn   10/10/ 2010

Growing Up with Listing to Lore Lyn 's Music.

As a child growing up, I like watching music stories on tv with mom. This lady came on name Lore Lyn and she sung this song (Coal Miners Daughter) 1 that was the first one of her songs I had hard. I wanted to listen to her songs all the time I remember when I would sing them with her on the radio, I really enjoyed hearing her sing. Like what her song was about real life, Lore said in her songs we didn't have much, but we had love. Herring her songs made me want to know more and to hear more of her song. What I heard was her life growing up with a large family as I did. My dad was a Farmer not a Coal Miner but both jobs was hard work. Like Lore said we have more them most people do and that the love of family. I wanted to go see her and Mom said you will when the time is right.

  Mom had enraged me and said one day I will. I hang onto my Dream after that one day that I would see her, day it was Picture time at School Mom fix up my Hair to look like hers.

I had tune 15 age and still in school. My hair was the hit at school that day. I want to be like her, Mom said you will one day. One hers and everyone at school like it. I felled like her that day.

I started to date this young man who lived across the Paint creek, we lived behind the P V School at this time in a big house. Lee and his Butte all came over, and we were listing to the radio and Lore came on singing the coal miner's daughter song and was listening to it then Lee tuned the station and said what you do that for, he said I don't like her, do you (yes) I ask why to put he didn't say. I had told him what my plans was one day was to go see her, after that I said no more about seeing her cause he wasn't interest in what I wanted. Now a lot of time has went by, and I had grown up. I'm still hanging on my Dream that one day I will see or meet Lore Lyn. The song (Love Flow) 2 came out.

I got Married in 1968 at the age of 17 a full week before I was 18, With my 1st. child. After we got marred Lee was working at a hog factory and as I started to get big for our baby he started to drink and getting drunk. He would go out with the boys a lot and the song (The Man of the House) 3 is never home he was always out somewhere with the Guys.

They all was out drinking and having fun and then the song (Don't Come Home with Love on your Mine)4 he came home smelling like a beer and with lipstick on him after playing around with other woman it is not the 1st times he's don't it before. While I was sick for our 1st. child born due, 1969 name Peewee, and we moved,

and I was due for our 2nd. 1971 name
Porky and as time went by, we were
having our 3rd child   the song came out
(Ones on the Way) 5, had come out.
Having kids Cuing Hungary and an
always wanting something you don't
have to give them. Not having the
money to get them what they wanted
or needed hurt me. I had felt that song
because I was doing all the housework
and the cooking what else that had to
be done. Caring for kids alone was a
hard job at time.it was time for our 3
child Lynn 1972 after she was born
into a full month the song (The Pill) 6
come out put I didn't want to take
anything that would kill a baby.

Now that more time went by, I was yet
to have one more child that made 4

kids after 6 months I was with a child
our 4th   1973 Jean was born, and she
was my last one and I didn't want
more. I got fixed when this song came
out (no more for me) xx

I saw the Coal Miners Daughter movie
came on and was watching felt like had
live her life. A lot of it story about Lore
was how my life was going. I had our 4
children, I was staying home and caring
for our kid's due for another baby
doing all the work taking care of our
kids. While the man of the house
drinks and out with his Buddy Friends.

Now a lot of time has when by and I'm
raising MY Kids alone which is how I
felt he is gone most of the time and we
needed extra money so me and the
kids would go out and pick up cans Lee

smoked and drink while I take care of
the kids . I had shared my Dream with
him only to get it shot down Lee didn't
believe in dreams and one day they
came Ture. So, I said no more about it
just went on dreaming by myself
thinking that I will one day prove him
Wrong. Now that all the kids were
born and growing up, I got a job to
help us.

 It's now 1975 and I'm working making
a little over $50. Dollars a week and I
don't smoke or drink. I wanted to save
up for a trip to take me and kids to the
Lore Lyn. place for some fishing and
horseback riding. I thought it would be
nice to take the kids to see her. Now I
continued to work different jobs but
couldn't save any money.it took a lot

to live on with only one income. The song came out (Mama He's Crazy) put I Change the title to Lazy it came out when he so lazy every time it came on, I sing with it and changed the words to lazy. And look at him.

Now after a full jobs and time has gone by me still have my Dream of seeing Lore and other dreams. But I know not to say anything because my old man doesn't care, he has always down me in what I wanted in life .I became angry and mad at myself, why I couldn't finger out, I worked all my life and had started to drink so much. But I still listen to Lore songs and Con way's where singing with her then and together they were good. Lore and Con way sang a lot of song that fit my story, like the one (Your Kids are Ugly) told a lot of how their Dad felt about his own kids. Lee didn't care for the music in which I liked He hated Con way didn't know why but the songs he sang said a lot about our life's.

I had bought some tickets to go see Lore at the Renfro Valley, KY. When I was working at the restaurant in Richmond Dale, I am planning this trip with a close friend Dou we were living together at this time ,we were going to rent a car and go there but money was a problem there was none to go. Now the restaurant I was working was closing their doors and I'm with out of a job2008 we moved to Chillicothe , on 4th street, I looked for work and got a job with the Sen Citizen Center as a dishwasher and cooks helper, with the help of a senior program who helps us get work. Work there for 3 years, until I fill and pass out dead gone.

2010 My tickets were about to expire, and I want so bad to go to this concert to see Lore Lyn, that year for my birthday. October 10 of 2010 was the concert, and Dou couldn't go he had no money to help get us there. I did get to go to the concert, how well I had a soon to be son in law Rick was going with Lynn, he went and traded some land for a Van and took me to Renfro Valley, KY. To see her. He didn't want to see the tickets go to waste which was $150. For 2 tickets and me not to get to see Lore Lyn. Was why I wanted to go?

Rick was the one who took me to the
concert to see Lore, we were gone for
a while the ride down was long, as was
the ride back. I was so very happy. the
next day I slept most the day cause the
ride tared me out. Rick and Lynn were
busy planning their wedding after that
Lee came by my house and said you
know what that looked like going down
there with Lynn boyfriend and I looked
back that him and said yes! I know it
looked like my dream came Ture at last
I got to see Lore Lyn in concert. And
Rick took me so to answer your
question yes, I know what it looks like
look like I got to go see her after all.
Thanks to Rick My son in law.

Hang on to your DREAMS they do
come TURE   Her 50th. Anniversary.

The happy ending of this story I got to
go see LORE LYN in Concert.   #1

By Jeannie Lynn/ of Waverly Oh.45690

   Taken at Renfro Valley KY. In front of
her Bus 10-10-2010. I got to go.
This one did come true for me.

 # 2. This Dream is of a house. I like to find some day!

I Jeannie was born in Santina, Oh. On Wilson Run Rd. on October 5 of 1950. To Dad and Mom. (Put I'm not Jack Kid.) Dark curly hair, brown eyes, and dark complexed skin. I was Born at 2; Am in the morning, a very likable child. I was a Blue Baby and wasn't expected to live, to see a day.

 My dream of a house I thought I was burned in was not me. The house was a big 3 store home with a basement in it the floors of this place was all Broken down

and the 3 floors was all in tacked
you could walk there.as I was
looking at things of this house I
found this picture of a small girl.
And on the back said dead 1950.
There was no month seeing this
picture and knowing who I was,
was surprising we look alike. The
outside of the house was white
with red shutter on all the
windows with a big rap around
porch. There were white post
pillars holding up the porch. And
flowers all the way around.

 There also was a fence in field in
front of this house with hogs in it
and a horse barn out back setting

in a slant with 5 nice looking horses , the one horse that stood out in my dream was the one little girl rode all the time the black one. The little girl at the age of 12 she died riding her horse and the horse died with her, they fell how I didn't get to see that part.

Put it was shocking to have it dream three time in a row, this feel like someone wants me to find this house. There was a log built well on the side of the house where they got water. This was a nice-looking working Farm.

Today I love horses and like to ride, and when I was born a blue baby and was told I wouldn't live pass the age of 12 got me thinking. Was I the girl on that horse and a copy of the little girl who died so I could live? That what got me thinking of reincarnating of one dying.

 Seen this dream I've been looking for this place. Something tells me it in Vinton country, So Dou. and I went to a road call park road and we tune left and sets a house that looked like what I was looking for. The man there said you can see it I said all I need to do is Put my

Hand on it and I will know if that it. The man said the house was build 1940. So, I got out and walked up to the house stepped on the porch. But that didn't tell me anything, so this was not the house.

 So, who was the girl age 12 died on the black horse and where did she live, her room of the house was on the third floor of this home?

 Pictures of me growing up look at the one where I was 6. /15/ 14

Whiten by Jeannie Lynn

Remember this was a Dream I had 3 time.

This Dream is of a house.

I'm still looking for this House.

3.Dream - of THE HAPPY PLACE
4-23.18

 I went to bed at 8; pm hurting in my body, and as I went to sleep, I started to have a Dream.

I was walking in the ally of Water Street in Chillicothe   and someone came out of a building there and was talking to me and wanted to know why I was unhappy. This person took me in this place I have never seen before. This place has 3 floors.

Inside this place was 5 offices of counselors to talk with you about what's bothering you. This place has all the common living arrangements starting with the 100 bedrooms underground to sleep in while you are there and bathrooms to accommodate all who stays there on the ground floor. On the floor above that was a Recreation center with bucket ball, tennis court, game room, and a lot more. And they have bands come there to play.

This is a place to get to know who you are and what you want out of life. The counselors help you understand yourself, help you find who you are, what you want to aconite!

There is a Cafeteria that is open all the time for thought who get hungry and just want a snack. They have Volunteer help come in and do all the cooking then they have the people in the program help serve the food if they want to. There are potty rooms on the other 2 floors.

You stay here until you are happy about yourself and you don't get out till you are. You want to find the out-side door till you are ready to leave. Wend I fine the door to go out I was in the ally of water street about 500 steps form paint street. I went to the light to cross them walk down a way to the ally of water street to an apartment I did not know I Live there. My thing was in there and I don't know how there got there and I work up form it Dream

 This place is a non-profit and gets help from all over. Be nice to see a place like this.

Dream by Jeanie Lynn

4.   Dream of a Wealthy Cowboy
4/27/18

I met this cowboy at my work, where I was working restaurant in Chillicothe, And I have 5 kids to raise and get thought school and not married. He acts me if I wanted a better life, so I act what do you have in mine. Then he took my phone number and later call me for an outing to talk.

He went on talking about this big farm and home he owned and want a woman to live there with him and take care of the house so he ack me to come with my kids and live in his house and be his women. He got 5000 acer farms with a big house.

There are lots of farm here, horse's
cow's pig's mules and others. He took
me on a golf cart around the farm
showing me everything and meeting all
the help and what they do. He wants
me to know everything about this
place.

The kids had the pick of any bedroom
the wanted. And me to. I got the next
door to his room. life here is good I got
anything and everything I wanted or
needed. New closed for the kids to
where to school. His said he loves kids
put couldn't have any. There were
housekeepers here and someone to
drive me any where I want to go. He
gave his card to the driver and the
driver was to go in every place I went,
for my protection.

This farm was somewhere of 35 closes to Greenfield. There 2 was in and there are 25 campers setting up on this place farm hands who took care of thing for this man. The lane went from front to the back where out. The back way was 35.

I didn't know his name. remember this was a dream.

Would like to find it Man.

Written my Jeannie Lynn

Dream of a Wealthy Cowboy
4/27/18

5.   This Story is about getting lost. (Lost and Not Knowing Who I am) 4-30-18

 This man I met name Roger
Somewhere on the Street ack me if I
wanted to go to a Carrousel   with him.
Well I said yes, I'll go not knowing who
he was and what was going to happen
after I got there so we road all the
rides there and play most of the games
there. We went in this big building he
wanted me to see and this was big.
After we was inside, we say everything
it was the weed Factory a place they
grow and pack and ship form. Then
this where we met Sue she works here
so she was of work and she node
Roger then we all started to walk
together until I got tared we came to

this sitting room and Sue said why
don't you set here, and we'll come
back for you, so I set down believing
then that they be back soon. yes, right
they went somewhere and forgot me, I
got up and started to walk the way I
saw then go in hopes

I would get up with then, put I could
not find then anywhere, I went down
these stairs and seen these big doors I
open them, and it was a bar and
people were drinking and smoking this
weed and having fun. At that time, I
back out of the bar, and started the
other way but this way went outside,
and I remember you need a key word
to get back in and did not know the
word You had to be with someone or
be a member, after I change my mine

and stayed inside I walk back to the
bar and went in walk thought it to the
other side and that side went outside
to. I didn't fine Roger or Sue, so I
assume they left me. I had no money
did not know where I come from and
did not know my name. so, what was I
to do?

 There was this truck driver and his
wife who saw me and seen I was lost
and on one with me, so they came
over to me and started to talk to me
and asking who I was put I couldn't tell
them, so they ask who you were here
with, so I name Roger and Sue you
have their last name. no, they didn't
say. So, the truck driver and his wife
took me with them to their place and
contacted the sheriff there   to find out

who I was and where I came from. so, I could go home. So, there was a DNA doing and pictures taken of me to see if anyone know me.

After it I don't know if I got home and still don't know me. I woke up.

Now remember it was a Dream.   By Jeannie Lynn

6.   Dreamers Paradise   6-21-18

I was driving down this street looking
around for a place, But I didn't know
what it was. Then I stopped and got
out then started to be walking to see
what I could fine. Put I still did not
know that what I was looking for.

I came to a place that looked run down
and empty It had a chain link fence
around it with locks on them and had
two big garage doors with locks also its
place was painted Green in the front.
so, I didn't know if I want to know
what this place was or not. Then across
the street was a parking lot and a big
car pulled in and it men got out .He
came across the street and saw me
looking at the building and ask who
you are and why I was looking at the

place. Then he replied you want to see inside; I wasn't sure what I wanted at that time. He begins to unlock the gate and the doors, when he opens then I was surprised at what I saw.

I when inside this place with him, Put I was still unsure, after the grange doors you would not believe the beauty of this place, this place has glass doors to go thought then he went on telling me why the look of the outside, so people wouldn't break out the windows. Now we're inside the place he had something to do then he going to show me around the place he is a very nice guy, I felt at es with him. He had Togo unlock the back doors for the help.

He got thing up a running, so he took me by the hand and said you ready to see it place my reply was yes let's do. We saw the bar as you walk in the place, and it has a restaurant in it and barber shop for man and women, there are other big rooms with lots of beds here for people to sleep, or nep and rooms for two people to go talk like a one on one. This place has a big kitchen and it helps the feed the homeless, they take in the homeless form the streets and anyone who have not nowhere to go.

So, I ask him why, lock the doors at night so no one gets hurt. Then he went on showing me the place, I said This look like a homeless place, and he reply it is somewhat. That was my mine purpose in starting this place was to help them. I ask how to do you pay

for this he said I use my own money to
be started and open the bar and
restaurant to the public who pays what
they can to eat. the pay here is
Donations. People bring in can foods
and freezer food other clothes,
furniture.

 He took me out back to see the
parking place where ones who have
cars and storage rooms for their thing.

There are people who come here to
talk to some of the people and help
them get back on their feet and back
to the outside living. So, I ask him what
if someone call in the night needing a
place to sleep, after you lock the doors
and gate. he replied I have a back way
in no one know about. I ask how you
can keep this place open, he replied I

us my own money to run it and with the restaurant the bar we open to the public.

 So, the morel of this story is a Home Away from Home All Cared for Here.

Now Remember this was a DREAM 6/21/18 by Jeannie Lynn

7. Farid of the Unknown 7/2/18

I was living in Chillicothe and working
at a restaurant in an Ally some where
there. The food storage and walk in
cooler was outside of this place, and
you need the keys for them. I was
going to the cooler to get some eggs to
put on to boil for Potato salad and on
my way there.

There was this Black pickup setting in
the parking lot with 2 guys in it. Look
like a dad and son. I didn't think much
about it; cause people sometimes do
this waiting on people. So not
watching them I went on to the cooler
with the key needed to get in. as I put
the key in the door to unlock it ,the
two men in the truck got out and
grabbed me broke the key of the

cooler took me back to their pick
up.one was a young man and the other
one was and older one this was a dad
and son team.

The young man said you will set on dad
lap; I said no I must work I can't go
anywhere with you. Then the young
man got out and put me in the truck.,
there was 3 other cars of people in the
parking lot and I was hoping they saw
what happened.

They started to drive I said ware we
are going I must work. I had no idea
why they took me or what for. So, we
went on a dirt road outside of town I
didn't get to see the sign we went on,
then up a hill to this big house. At the
house was a lot of people and they

looked like drunks and druggy they were all silly looking.

These people didn't care at what was happing they was having a Party. I kept saying I need to go back to work, they said you'll be working soon. One of then put a needle in my arm and said this will coma you down. So, at that point I know where and what I was there for DRUG Lords house to hook and sale. There was this one guy came in a Big blue car, looked at me and said she'll do, then one of the others told him she's a cook. Somehow a lady cop showed up at this place and she looked at me and was going to arrest me for using drugs, and I had told her these people here kidnap me and brought me here then put a needle in my arm.

Look like someone saw what was going
on and called the cops then followed
the truck to tell then where I was at.
Thank God.

So, she started to look around this
place then called for backup. I think
she saw something or someone who
was missing for some time.

Then I was taken home to my place in
town, my sister was there, and the cop
walked me to the door. Kay ask what
had happen and the cop told her
where she found me, put kay wasn't
surprised .the cop was going to my job
to let them know what had happened
and that it will be two weeks before
she'll be back to work. After the cop
left kay tried to coma me down put, I
was still afraid of what had happened

to me. I would get under the dresser and hide; I wouldn't come out. It took me two weeks to recover from this and to get back to myself. I went to counseling for help.

I went to my job they said we can't have you back here, we hired someone else for your job Sorry. Then I walk out of the restaurant disappointed about my job because I know I had doing anything wrong.

Now I have no Job, they think I'm a drug user, but I'm not. My rent is coming due soon and no money coming in I want to be able to pay my bills and nowhere to go.

I can't go to my kids they hate me and don't want me around.

 So, the moral of this story: Watch your surrounding if someone is setting around in a parking lot and look like there waiting for someone they are, there looking for a new person to take advantage of (That You)

Remember this was a DREAM. By Jeannie Lynn

.

8 Dreams of Wolves &
Coyotes with Wild Cats   7/13/18

I went to this river boat
restaurant to eat because
everyone was saying it was a
good place to eat. Then ones I got
there I needed to use the rest
room, so I went into the
restroom, put it was so dirty with
shit piss all over it the floors,
seats, and counter. There was on
wear it was clean. I saw this white
door and I went in it; I just
needed a place to scoot to piss
that's all.

Then I went back into the restaurant and there were no seats it was all filled up of people. There was this one man setting at a table by himself and he ask if I would like to join him for dinner. He was in a wheelchair, I had seen him on TV before, but I couldn't remember who he was then he went on to tell me his name.

My name is Brad Wry, then I told him who I was, but I wasn't nobody like he was. He said that ok we are just having dinner together. We order dinner and before we saw bunches of wild looking cats and dogs, wolfs surrounding the place. there was a cat under the table, and it bit me on the leg brad made it go away, but the more we fight it got aggressive came back. Outside there were more big dogs coming around the place and looking mad. The manager opens the doors of the restaurant because it was getting hot in the place, so he didn't see the dogs and cats surrounding the place. Soon the wolf like dogs and cats came into the place and started to bit people who was eating. They were everywhere there was no getting away form then.

People was running to their cars
trucks any anywhere they could
to get away from the animals.
Brad had a Bus out in the parking
lot put it was too far away to get
with a wheelchair, so we went up
to the top of this Boat building, to
get away from them. Then after I
got him to a safe at the top ,I saw
this lady with 3 children trying to
get her family out of the way of
the wolfs, then I went back down
and got them then brought then
back up to the top of the boat
where we were at.

I closed the door behind us, and
we all were safe there. So, we

waited it out until it got late then
Brad looked out the upstairs
window and it had look like all
was safe to go the wolfs and
other animals had left. We all
went back downstairs to our cars.
I help the lady with her kids then
they were on their way home.
Then I help Brad to his bus, then
his people who was with him
came out and got him on the bus.
Then I went to find my car put it
was gone look like someone had
taking it put how, I had the keys.

Brad had a driver and he's band
on the bus, so they were safe, this
one man got the lift down and

lifted Brad into the bus, Brad's
people were watching me and
told him she can't find her car.
Look like she alone. Then Brad
had one of his people bring me
abroad his bus, then Brad ask me
you have anyone to go home to, I
said no why, why don't you come
with me, I could use your help.
And someone to talk to. Then he
went on to saying come on and
let's get out of here. He knows I
was wet cold and tried from all
we went thought so he got me
one of his t-shirts and had me go
lay down in his bed for a while. I
must have been tried because it

was Morning went, I awoke. It was getting late so Brad did lay beside me and sleep to.

The next morning Brad ask me if you have anyone waiting for you at home Why don't you come stay with me. We all would love it then he asks me what I like doing, so I told him I love to Cook. And that was all he needed to hear. He had his people go to my place and get my thing then he said what you don't have we will buy for you.

Remember this is a DREAM by Jeannie Lynn #8

9. The Dream of a Flea Market
7-14-18.

I worked for this family who sets up on weekends Saturday and Sunday to sale their new items at Flea Markets. They ask me if I wanted to set up with them to sale my homemade crafts and a full of my what nots I gather over the years. I had my thing in a trailer then these people went and got my thing from these trailers and put them in their big box truck. Then they went on to the Market and set up there thing and my thing to sale. My thought was they are trying to control me,

that was in my mine. After I got
their house cleaned and my job
here was done. I went to this Flea
Market to see where my thing
was setting at and if they were
selling anything.

Ones I got there I saw my thing
among there thing and people
was looking at these things I
made look like people was looking
at my thing put I didn't see all the
thing I had sent with them.

The coming Sunday at the flea
market I went to the office there
to see if I could get my own
space. They said I had some

marks again me and I didn't have a job. Then I said what's having a job got to do with the Flea Market.

Then I told them I was retired 67 years old lady who on SSA. disable. then they still said that I was not allowed to get my own space.

Then I got my pickup and went to back to the flea market with boxes to pack my thing. Put the people who had my thing already packed and left with my thing.

I know where they live so I'm going there to get what was my thing, or what was left of them. These people were not at home with the truck, so I couldn't get them. They had taken off to anther flea market for the following weekend. Put I wasn't informed as to where. Now I'm waiting to see what happen to my thing.

Now as a full day has pass and these people hasn't contacted me as to where they are put, they do have my mailing address, so they can write me and let me know something and when there'll be back. Later in the mail a letter came from them they were on

there was back and that they had
good news for me and there was
going to help me. Them they ask
if I would go to the house and
clean it for their home coming.
Then I did go there and got thing
ready for then, and while I was
there, they came home, then they
had written me two checks one
for the cleaning $300. And one for
the thing they sold for me was
$700.dollars.

Then they wanted to know if I
could make more of the murals
and handbags, I said yes how
many more are you thinking. They
went on telling me of the good

news they had to tell me. People wanted all your murals and handbags; they want more all you can make. Then these people took orders for my home-made crafts, now I have work to do.

They went out and rented a big building for me to work in and they got me everything to work with. Then they wanted to get me help to work with me. They had an order for 150 murals, and handbags to match. So that was 300 pc. Of the crafts to make. I didn't know what to say the orders didn't stop there these people had set up a web site for

my crafts and the orders kept
coming in.my job as crafts maker
was getting bigger and I was
loving it.

Because of these people I now
have a good job and I'm selling
my work online. Thank you,
People, whoever you are for
believing in me and helping my
crafts get out there for people to
enjoy.

 Remember this was a DREAM, By
Jeannie Lynn

 I do make Murals, and Hand
totes to sale Among another thing

#10. The Wish Class 7-18-18

The School started a Wish Class,
they had 30 kids in their
classroom and this class was 1
day a week. The kids in Class
was asking to write down 5
wishes, that they want for their
self's or their family. This class
was in hope to out things like
what some family needed in
their home life and what their
kids needed for school. Thing
that they couldn't afford to get
them. Things like new Shoes,

Clothes, paper and pencils thing they use daily.

All the kids went to this class it wasn't mandatory, but the kids saw it as getting the change of getting thing they wanted or needed. All the kids had it class who wanted it. I'm not sure which school started this class put this a good one. There was a church in with it class. These wishes listed was given to a Church group was they would make wishes come Ture. The people would go out and buy these things for these kids who wanted things like warm coat, new shoes and socks, a new outfit for school. Things like Food for a family help with Paying bills.

There was this one girl who want to be a writer and her family could afford paper and pencils for her to do it. This was one of her wishes, to have what she needed to write. Then the following weekend someone came to her home brought her paper and pencils to work with and a gift card of $5000. Dollars to get more when she need it and to use on publishing her book. that was one girl wish had come True.

There was this boy who said my family is poor, and that we don't get new shoes or coats for school. Then after a full week this boy 's family was taken by surprise; someone came to their home with Boxes of things like new shoes coats for the whole family. That wasn't all they got they got food and other thing needed for their home, like blankets, towel. For this Boy, his wish came Ture.

Then there was this Boy who
wanted for his family, to make
extra money so they could pay
their bill's. They were going to
be put out of their home
because they couldn't pay the
rent or utilities for the place.
Then a full week went by and the
following week something
happened. this family got
$200,000. Dollars. they were
able to pay off their bill's and
keep their home. There lifts got
better after that the man of the
home got a job and was making
good money. Anther Boy's wish
come Ture.

Most of these kids wishes was
granted and there were lots of
happy kids because of this Class.
A Church somewhere was
helping to make these wishes
come Ture for these kids.

Thank you, GOD, for these kids.

Remember this was a DREAM, by
Jeannie Lynn

Share your Dream's Write them
down and put them in a book.
some where someone may need
to read this.

I went looking for a Job and a Place to
live with my 4 children's, I came
across this apartment and went
inside to look around then its man
came out to talk to me and wanted to
know what I was looking for. I told
him that I was looking for work and a
home for Me and my kids, then he
asks how many kids I replied 4, then
he asks a full more?? What kinds of
work have you done, cook and
cleaning I'm a sewer I like making
crafts, and I'm a letter Mailer, and
that all he needed to here?

Then he went on telling me about his
self and how he works out of town as

a truck driver A lot and that he needed someone to care for this place that can be here all the time he is a very nice man. Being all men with some being women that didn't bother me, we all had locks on our doors We beep holes.

Then he asks me if I wanted the job, and a place to live he said you and the kids can stay here and I'll pay you $500. Week for taking care of the place. Then he said remember it mostly men who lives here. Their truck drivers and road workers, some of them meet there wife here. Then some are not with anyone then he said are you ok with that, then I said yes, I'm fine with that

Then he said you and your kids have
the 1ˢᵗ.floor living there 10 rooms
there a kitchen washroom with 3 sets
of washers and dryers. For everyone.
There were 25 extra rooms in this
place. Almost all full. And yes, there
was some women here too.

Then my girls and boys picked their
rooms. And my room was behind the
office all had their own bathrooms,
so neon had to leave their rooms. My
job was to cook for the men and
Clean their rooms and keep thing
quitted. For them cause some of the
slept for the day. My kids were in
school during the day and didn't get
home till $pm. While they were in
school, I went to my sewing room to
start my days' work, I could see the

counter door form where I was at. So, if someone came in, I would know it.

The Kitchen was big, and the dining room was too, then I cooked for the ones who ordered breakfast the night before and some extra for those who forgot, I had made

 Plenty of food. When dinner was ready a lot of the men eat with use, which made a nice time, talking about what they wanted to do. Then after the guys took some to their rooms for later eating. My kids all got peeper so when I needed them while they were home, I could call them to help with some of the shores. Like dishes sweeping and mopping up.

All the workers understood about the kids and they were all good to them, they talked to them about thing kids wanted to know. Me I worked a lot in my sewing room and some of the men needed something mended then I fix them for them.

I did my work in this building that needed doing, kept clean towels and bedding in all the rooms, most the men in here helped a lot by keeping their rooms cleaned for me.

When the mane manager came in, he was most satisfied to how thing was done, then, he said you are doing a good job. Then he went on to say I'm going to give to you bones all the men here took up for you a little extra cash, $1000. Dollars, then I took my kids out to eat and shopping, for some new thing. Then got me some new Sewing and lettering thing so I have thing to work with.

I didn't get this man name just that he was very nice, and good looking and he love kids, he didn't have any of his own. The kids I believe was Mine.

Remember this was a DREAM by Jeannie Lynn.

#12. The Beach Party W/ Sharks
7-25-18

There was this place that had a mountain by it. We went around it to get to the Beach, 5five of use girls we were sisters and I was surprised that we got along. Because before we didn't. Ones we got to the Beach we unpacked our thing form the van. We set up our Tents and sleeping bags, because we were going to be there for a week. After we was don't setting up everything. We got in our swim wear, to go swimming.

There was an older couple there setting on the Beach and they said you can't go in that water then we ask WHY, it not safe. Then they went on saying there a big Shark in there and he's watching for people. Well we didn't believe them so one of us went in the waters nothing happened.

Put after seeing that we waited for a while she played out there, then we all went in the waters. We were playing in the waters then the couple was sitting on the Beach watching, they told us it wasn't safe. Two big Sharks came up in the waters and we ran out of the waters. We did stay at the Beach for two more days doing other thing, like hunting shells in the sand.

The older couple had left the Beach so that left us alone here. We were spending out 2nd. Night here on the beach we all tuned in to sleep for we were going to leave the next day and we want to rest up. We packed our thing that night. Now that its morning the water was up around our camp site. We didn't see the

Sharks anywhere, yet we all looked. They were waiting until we got up to make there move.

The Van parked was too far away to just make a run for it. We had all packed up our thing the night before because we were leaving the next day.

The older couple that was there when we got there came back with help lifeguard to check on us. And Thank God they did, the Sharks was waiting to get us. Then the Guards helped us of the Beach, and we were on our way home. We did Thank the older couple and the Guards for their help.

 The Moral of this story is when someone tells you something is not safe listen. And don't do it. Most older people have been there.

Remember this was a Dream by Jeannie Lynn

#13. Grandma Old Sewing Machine. 7-30-18

I went to my Grandma home a lot and she was sewing on this old sewing machine, she had two of them. She let me us one of them to learn how to sew, grandma was teaching me how to put a guilt together with it. Then she went on talking about how her mom teach her how to sew, and that her Mom used the machine that she is letting me use. She said that was the first one I used to learn on that one was Mom's machine. This one had a big black box over it then Grandma said that one an older one that how they first came out. The Table it was on was lovely with drawer and black paddle under it. Anywhere while I was at grandma's house, she had its lady come by to talk to me. She wanted to know more about what I wanted to make using the machine.

I told her I like to learn to make what grandma making quilts and murals you hang on wall's, tote bags, table mats. Then after she left grandma made an

appointment for her to come
back as my teacher to help me
learn to sew. Grandma know of a
quilting show in town and
wanted me to have one in it.
After the teacher left grandma
went on teaching me how to
work the sewing machine so I
would be ready. She got both
machines' out and ready to us.

My first lesson was the following
Monday and Grandma went out
and got me some new Material
for the new quilt I was going to
make for the show. Then the
Lady came for my lesson that

Monday, and grandma was baking pie's and cooking, she was staying out of the way, so the teacher could do what she was getting payed for. My first class went good and Grandma was pleased.

The teacher was coming three days a week. For 5 weeks because grandma wanted me ready for the quilting show. After the Lady left each day me and Grandma would go on sewing on the quilt, so she was teaching me too. Then she said we need to get you a new dress, and I told grandma I like to make me a Sack dress, then she got an ideal let's make you a quilted dress. Yes, Grandma I'd like that. Then she went out and got more material for the dress she wanted me in Blue. So, we went on with my sewing classes, and I was learning a lot fast. Grandma and I was putting my quilt together for the show thing was coming together. Ones we got the quilt done we work on my dress she said we'll put the square together and then cut it out, in your size then put lace on it.

I was being to like this sewing
thing and I wanted to know
more about how, then she was
teaching me all she could then
we started to write down my
question about sewing so we
could ack the teacher. It was
about time for the showing of
our quilts and we were ready,
then something happened
grandma got sick laid in bed and
couldn't go to the show. But she
said your teacher is taking you to
the show and she'll be there
with you, now you take mine
and your quilt. My quilt came in
2nd. And grandma came in first

place. My dress was a hit made with three shades of blue. I had two of these best teachers. She was proud of me.

She had a will made out and I was to get the sewing thing and both machines. My Grandma got more sicker and I know she was leaving me.

My Grandma I loved so much has died, she left me all her sewing thing to me. But I didn't have a way to haul then home with me. I know some family members who had a truck, then I ask them if they would help me

being these things to my home.
They hadn't answer me yet, so I
was thinking they needed to find
help.

These people went to my
Grandma house and took
everything in it including my
machines. Stole all of it and sold
to and action somewhere. I want
to find these people who took
from the dead, thing they had
known right to.   #13.

The moral of this Story is Don't
trust anyone including you
family they will steal form you.
And don't tell someone that the

member has just die, and there no one that the house. Thieve are looking for these places.

Remember this was a Dream by Jeannie Lynn.

Share your Dreams it just might be what they need in their life's.

14. The Mobil Veterinarian 8-2-18

I have a small dog that got hit on the
road, she got her hip broken. I call
the veterinarian all over to come out.
But no one makes house calls and I
didn't have a way to take her to
them. Them someone know someone
who did make house calls. She had a
Mobil unit she come out in it. I called
her, and she came out to care for my
dog. Then she went on saying how
and why she started this Mobil unit.

She said people had a lot of small
animal like you who don't have a way
to get them to a Veterinarian office,
to get the help needed. I wanted to
help thought people get that help,
there a lot of people who needs their

dogs, cats fixed to bring down unwanted animals. She went on saying that she was looking for someone to travel with her to help her with her work. She wanted someone who help cared for the animals like nursing.

She got calls to go all and around the states to care for their animals. This sound like something I like to do. She said you can come with me your dog will need to stay with me anyway for more care. Then she said why don't you come with me on some of these trips and see if it is something you like. If you don't like it, I will bring you back.

She went on saying she had to go into town and get supplies for her work. She bought me home for a full day and I give this some thought. I did enjoy helping her with this work. Then while she was in town getting supplies for this work.

I give this some thought and ask myself what was keeping me here and she did say I could bring my dog. While she was going, I put something together to go with her. She stops back to check on my dog. I asked her if she was serious about this job of traveling on the road and working with you, she said yes are you in.

She was hoping I would come with her, she said I was a lot of help to her.

So, I did go with her, I had nothing
keeping me here or form doing that.
No one here who needs me but my
dog, and I can take her with me. Do
the thing you love doing.

15. The New Drinking Club.

8-5-18

There was a new place opening in town called a drinking Joint. People say this for nondrinker to go and have some fun. This place had a dance floor and pool table, games to play with there was something for everyone here. There was a jot box with old and new Music and live bands there to. This place didn't service alcohol of any kind, it purpose was to open to sober and nondrinkers.

They service Pop, Juice, Coffee, Tea, and top Shell sparkle Drinks. This place has vending machine for your Smacks like Chips, candy bars, and we have Sandwiches of all kinds. In this place no one fight there no arguing here it not aloud.

This place look like a big barn with lots of room to move around and it had rooms of the to the side if you needed to talk. This place set up two times a week for a soup kitchen for the homeless, they give clothes and food away to the needed. People

who could come here would
bring thing for them.

This place is looking for kitchen
and waitress help.

By this time, I woke up, and
didn't get the ending of this one,
so I hope you get and Ideal or
something from this one.

 Remember this was a Dream
from the Night. 8-5-18

By Jeannie Lynn,

Remember to Share your
Dreams it may help someone

16. Lost at the Gambling Hall
8-26-18

I was with this man I was going with and he wanted to go see if he could win some money. Me I'm not much on the slot machine so I stay in the TV room watching the horse racing. he had given me $3.00 if I needed a smack or something to drink. But my thought was it isn't going to buy anything here.

The TV room was next to the slot room where he was playing. But I couldn't see him in there. There was a lot of people in there.

Sound like people was wining. I went to the door to see if I could see him, but I couldn't.

I needed to go find the restroom, so I went looking for one. I didn't know the place and I got lost, did find a restroom by asking someone. When I was ready to go back to the TV room I had just came from. I didn't find it. So, I stopped by this vending machine was going to get me a bag of Chips. But they were more than I had money for $3. Dollars was going to buy anything here, so I didn't get anything.

I still didn't fine the TV room where I was supported to be. When he got done playing the slots machines.

I was getting more lost currently, and there were these people going around shooting doors to these rooms. Then I ask someone what time it is. "They said closing time."

So, I still hadn't found the man who I came here with I was lost and believed left behind. So, I started to walk again to see if I could spot him. But I never did.

Then I sat down not knowing what to do. I was tried, scared and hungry. I felt that I was left. Then it one color guy sat down beside me and saw I was crying by the man who bought me here. He wanted to know why I was still here. Everyone else had gone. I told him how I got there but the one who brought me here left me. I didn't know what to do and I had no way home.

Then this man sitting here listened to me, he said come

with me we have an extra room you can sleep, and my wife will make you something to eat. Then tomorrow we'll take you back to your place or wherever you want to go.

So, I went home with him and he said don't worry you be fine. Then he called his wife and told her that he was bringing me to their home. His wife was getting supper and she had sat 3 plates, knowing he was bringing me. They took care of me and made me feel welcome in their home.

His wife made up the guest room for me.

When I got up the next morning, she had my breakfast ready and I eat. Then they were both was ready to take me home to Chillicothe. I went to my sister in laws place. She knows me better then I know myself. Now I'm back home, she took care of me from then on. Then she wanted to know what happen. I told her. She didn't have any good words for the snake who would do something like that.

She did know who I was going with, so we went there, and he wasn't home and hadn't come home. So, we got my thing form his house and put them in storage then I stayed with her for a while.

Then we finely find me my own place. I said never again will I do that again, **that was Scary and Crazy trip for me**.

 Remember this was a DREAM, by Jeannie Lynn

Hope you get something from these Dreams.

17 Lost and Found 8-28-18.

I was wondering down the road in my
pickup. I came across a closed
mountain. I stop to look at it because
it looked different them most I have
seen. It looked like a hole in a wall
there was something about it at
didn't seem right. Outside of it look
like a junk yard or someone had just
left the cars.

Then I went looking around I saw that
someone made an entry was inside. I
looked inside, and you want to
believe what I saw. There was 5
people living here in this hole. "It was
Sad."

Then I started talking to them why
they were there, my thought was

they was site seeing as I was. There answer was no we got stuck here then I ask how? There mountain came down on use while we were there, and we couldn't get out.

Then I ask who made the doorway, the two men there said we did so we could get out and fine food. Then my next thought was why did you not go home, we couldn't our cars was buried.

We all were under this mountain, so we all stayed here hoping someone would come and help use, put no one came.so the men went hunting for food, they all work together caring for each other. These people were lost to the outside life.

Now about the people in the mountain there was this older man and women married couple and a young couple with a two-year-old with them, who is now ten years old. Some where someone is missing a son, he was caught here to. He was eight-year-old when he went missing. His family is out there somewhere looking for him. Then there this Elderly lady who was walking and full of energy is now not able to do anything.

This older man and women took care of her, and the young couple card for the of both kids. These people been here for better than eight years now. So, when I went in and asked, what can I do to help you. They said there was five other people here who said the same thing but on one came back here to help use.

Then I went to my car and made a full phone call. I had people coming to help them, Squad, Van to take all them to the hospital for checkups. They were so happy to finely get some help. Then after that they went to a shelter home for a full day.

Then I got the missing posters book and was looking for this boy who went missing so I could find his family. I found the missing boys' picture in the book and got an address where they were living. I went there but didn't find them, the people there bought the house said they left town.

Then I went to the Sheriff's office there told them about this child whom I found. Then they went to working on his case. They did find the boy's dad, but his mom had died. His dad didn't want him, so he stayed with the only people whom he knows. The elderly lady went to the nursing home and was cared for there where she stayed.

Now the families are all back among the living. Thank You God.

I have one question, what would you have done for these people who been lost from life for so long? Think about this!

18. The Fungai Treatment Center   9-7-18

I was working for this Factory and I
used the water there to wash my
hands. I was there little over a year
working. Some of the other people
there was getting laid off why I didn't
know. No one was talking about this.
While I was working here, I notice
that my fingernails were coming off,
and my hair is fulling out. Then my
skin started to peel off. I didn't know
why this was happening.

I called my Doctor and got an
appointment, got one in two weeks
to see her. Then she looked at me
and know what was wrong with me.
You have Fungal deices and then I ask

what that she went on telling me you get this from water, washing your hands in bad water. Taking a shower in your home with bad water. You will lose your hair, nails, and skin. She went on telling me that I will need to go to a Fungai Treatment Center that takes care of people with this deices. This place was here closet to home. She was going to set this up for me to go there.

Then I went to my workplace at the Factory told them what I was doing, then they laid me off. So now I know now why people was getting laid off. They must have got It to like I did. Now I was home with no job to come back to. Now I have a deices of Fungai.

I got up the next morning, went into
to this small town and there was this
small restaurant there, so I stopped
in there for Breakfast. My hands were
peeling bad I had them warped up
and got some big Gloves on them.

There was a woman running this
place said I know you didn't you work
in restaurants, I said YES. Then she
asks if I would work for her.

I went on telling her why I couldn't
help her. put she assured me you will
have a job here when you get back
from treatment. I went back home
getting thing ready for my treatment,
and to get thing together as to what I
was taking with me.

Now I'm on my way to the Treatment
Deices Center, they put me in a room
of my own. I didn't know how I was
going to pay for this, then they ask
was you working at this Factory when
this happened, YES, I was. The doctor
there said the Factory is paying this
BILL. I was not to worry about this
just get Well.

There was this Pill they give you five
times a day, and a body wash you use
to treat this. Now I'm getting the
treatment and help needed for this
thing. I'm there for around four
weeks for this and was getting better.
Then they went on telling me you
don't have to worry about money
then I ask Why.

I saw others there who had work at the Factory to and that why they got laid off to. Because of the water there. No one could speak off the treatment there.

The Factory I was working ware I got the deices from, must pay you $300.weekly for the rest of your life. Which was your weekly paid. Because it was there that you are here. It was there water that put you in this shape. Now I set for Life with money coming in.

Now my Treatment is done and I'm going home. I stop by this little restaurant to see the lady in charge off this place, I ask her was you still wanting me to work for you. she said

Yes, I told you this job was here waiting for you if you want it. She had kept her word and I said YES, I want it.

I went on home took a good look at myself. I liked what I saw my hair, nails. And skin was back and better looking. I was getting back what I had lost.

Now I'm a new me again I still have a Home. Job and Income and my Life back.

THANK GOD

Remember This was a DREAM   Not Real.

Written by Jeannie Lynn.

19. Bingo Train Ride   9-11-18.

Connie and I was going to go on this
Train to play Bingo. This Train Ride
Costed us $250 each for the two
night plus for food and drinks, and
the scratch off tickets. We took our
saving and went together for the
ride.

This Train had seats where you sat
across from each other it had tables
that came down in front of you to us.
While you are playing. Our first night
which was Friday starting at 5 pm we
were on. We were booked for two
nights; Saturday and you must
remember the number and train car
and seat you on from the night
before. Cause someone from the

Train call out the number of the car and you better be at the doors when it opens.

Anyway, our first night on the bingo Train we played bingo and the tickets. We were winning back what we had spent to get on the train. The Train was moving down the tracks where we went, I didn't know because no one got off. The train had stopped for break and we went to the restroom which was in the car we were on. So, no one had to go far to use it. We got our snack lunch and went back to our seats to eat.

After the break, the train was back to moving and everyone was playing again. It wasn't long after the break the game was over for the night. We were taken back where we started to where we got on. The parking lots. The people of the train said we'll see you all tomorrow night. Which was our 2nd Night Saturday like I said before you are to remember your car and seat number.

Now we are back for our 2nd night of fun. Playing and winning bingo. We were moving and this time I was watching were we was going. I opened the curtain of the train. We went to a part of town I Haden seen before it was petty there. Connie looked to and saw it. She didn't know it.

We were winning back the money we took with use. Then Connie and I said we want to do it again. This was a lot of fun I enjoyed it. Then we all got our break and our snacks for that evening. We had spent most of what we went with there.

This game night was about over, and I said to Connie that the most fun I've had in a long time then she said we'll do this again. Now the train has come back to where we all started, and it was time for use to get off.

 Then the people who works the Bingo Train Ride ask if everyone had fun then as we were getting off, they handed us flyers for the next Bingo Train Ride. I was listening the some of the other people who went on it ride complaint they had loss their ass, or all their money and wasn't happy.

Connie and I came of the ride with what we took on we watch what we spent on our 2nd night so we wouldn't be brock. Which was a good thing at it points.

As we went to get off the Train, we didn't see the car we came there in, the one we left in the parking lot. Now how was we going to get home. Connie had her cell phone with her, so she calls someone to pick us up. Went we got home there set her car at the house we left in the parking lot. Connie was mad that someone took the car from the lot. She asks how my car got home before I did. Her son went and got it said he needed to use it. Then Connie ask how you started it, then he said I have a key. Where did you get a key no one else is supposed to have a key?

Her son went and had one made without her knowing he had done this.

The moral of this story is making sure who holds your keys is not going to make copies of your keys remember you keep your house keys on that ring. Others can take what you have while you are gone out of town.

Well we are home now and back to
what we were doing before The
Bingo Train Ride.

 Remember this was a DREAM   not
real...

By Jeannie Lynn.

20. The Wicked Weather   9- 15-18

I went to town and it was raining
Bad just coming down. I was meeting
my Sis for Lunch at this one big Store
this has a Restaurant in it. My Sis and
I when in and sat down that this
table, then we were going to order
our food. But before someone game
out and said we sent the help home
we must close the restaurant, the
mountain in back is coming down. So,
we got up to leave and before the
manger give use a bag of chips and a
drink. As we were leaving the
restaurant it had blowing up the
crash came into it and went boom.
We look back then we ran to another
part of the store. We came to it
sitting room and there were other

people in here talking about this weather. They were saying that something was going to happen to this town.

I got up and went looking for a restroom to use. The others stayed in the room with my Sis, was still sitting in the room. Soon as I left for the restroom a big machinery came down from the bank then and mud came in that room it covered everyone with mud the machinery had crash then all. I went back to see it but couldn't get in.

The alarm went off then the doors was closing thought out the building. I started running to get out of it, so I wouldn't be trapped there. There were other people in here, but they didn't seem worried. But they didn't see what I saw.

The restaurant, blowing up. And my sis covered with mud. I was afraid what else was going to happen here.

I got to the outdoor, but it was closed I couldn't get outside. Then someone came up to me and said you'll better off in here. Then I ask what you say, you know it building is fulling down. The man said Yes, but there one room here we can all be safe Then he took me there. He had taken a lot of people to this room; he calls this his safety net room. He said it isn't the 1st time this happen. Then he went on saying nothing will happen here you are safe in here. Then I ask how we will get out when the Strom over. Then he said trust me everyone stay com.

Now the Storms over, we all got out the man had a secret hole to the outside. Now we are all out, but the town was a Deserted. We all went looking for our cars put they was gone junked. So now what to do I stood there thinking my home is not that far out. So, I started walking home. Then a lot of the others was doing the same walking home.

I could see my house and it was still standing which was a good thing. When I got there, I went inside and found that someone had taking some

of my thing's. But there was nothing I
could do about it right now. I was
tired, scared wet and dirty all I
wanted to do was get a bath and
some rest on my bed. So, at this time
that what I did. I laid me down to
sleep I slept   the hole day.

When I got up, I was going to get me
something to eat. Then there was a
knock at my door it was some of my
neighbor's they had nowhere to go
home to no food and no beds. Then I
saw they was like me when I got
home. But I had a home to come to
and food, bed to sleep. So, I let then
in and I was getting dinner for myself
then I ask them you want to eat
Dinner with me. They said Yes, we
will then I had them go take a bath

and come back down then dinner will be ready.

Seem they had nowhere to go home to, I had this big five-bedroom home not being used so I had them stay here until they could find out about their place.

So, they stay here with me.

Then the Hospital called the next day we have your Sis here with us, You what. I saw her die with the others in the land fill that hit the building. They said no she here and alive. Sis had to stay there for a while the scare of this has her down bad. The next day I walk in town to the hospital to see her. She said I want to come home with you, can I go home with you, I said Yes Sis you can come home with me. So, the hospital releases her to me, and we went walking home. She was ok after that we was home

I give her one of the bedrooms with the bathroom in it, so she could have her own. She was still a little scared, hell I was to be thinking I had lost her. I'm grateful she well and here with me home.

The hole town was lost gone, but we still had a few thing's Bank and Hospital there. There was no Store's.

My life and my Sis, and Neighbor 's was all ok. We're all well and living at my place. Remember this was a DREAM not real.   By Jeannie Lynn.

21. Homeless and Hungary
9-18-18

I was living in this big house with lots of bedrooms in an Alley Way. Where it seems like it was under a bridge like. This place had 6 bedrooms, and I was living there with my husband at this time. Then suddenly he died how I didn't know. But he left everything to me here, house, and money.

This place I was seeing all the people coming and going in this Alley Way, there was looking in garbage cans for food and setting in doorways of these businesses.

They looked like they needed someone to help them.

Then I went to talked to some of them about why they were out here. They said we have nowhere to go then I asked. How have you been eating they said from what people would put in the trash cans.

After talking to some of them I went back to my house and then I started thinking about how I can help them.

I went to the Community Center
there and was talking to them,
they said there have been trying
to work with them put there was
more them then they could do
for. These people there said
these people needed Shelter,
Food put we have not been able
to get to all them.

Then this one Man went on
telling me, what could be done if
they had the money to do it.
There is this old School House
Building setting empty and lots
of rooms we could make a
Shelter out of it. Then they could

sleep in and kitchen to cook in, to feed them. After talking with them I got to thinking about how I can help them. I live where some of them do in the Alley Way. I can cook up a lot of foods and have them in my home. I could make up some Sack lunches for them to. I have the money I can do this for them, because I was left with my husband money.

I went to the Grocery Store to get something, so I could do this with, and I saw the five carts setting in a row with a lot of can foods in it. Price on the carts say $250. Dollars, this storekeeper came over while I was looking, and I asked how much for all five carts. She let me have them for $150. After what I told her what I was doing. I got all five carts and had help to load the can food.

Then I went looking for hand can openers to give the people, so they could open them and heat them up to eat. I gave all these people 3 cans of food each as they came to my door along with their sack lunch, I made them.

There was a lot of them, and I found a way I could help feed them. I did there was more and more of them coming to my door the word got out there. I was giving food away so that got more people to my door I was doing this by myself.

Then there was these three homeless ladies' who look like they could use a bath, and some clean clothes so I ask them if they wanted to come in and wash up a little. They said Yes, we haven't had a bath in eight months that was my 1st guess to

the bathroom. There was three
bathrooms in this house.

Now I found another way I could
help these people. Then I went
to yard sales thought out this
town looking for clothes. shoes
boot anything they could wear. I
went to Walmart to get new
under wear for both man and
women. I only gave the clothes
after their bath.

I have a washer and Dryer where
I could keep their clothes clean. I
had them put there thing in a
bag with their name on them
then I wash them by their selves.

Now I'm feeding them and allowing them to take a bath and washing their clothes.

I have a big living room with lots of seating, so if one of them wanted to talk we'd go the front room.

I'd made coffee and cakes we could have. then after I found yet another way, I could help them. Having someone to talk to mean a lot to them. I listen to what they said about thing and how they got to it point in their life's.

Then I went in town to speak to someone about coming to the house and counselor them in my home. Now I got that set up then they all had thing to say. The coworkers went to working on their cases finding out why they were homeless.

Then she had people coming to take them to Doctors for checkups. They took them to the welfare offices for Aid and food stamp, then they went to the Section-8 department to find them homes. A lot of them was living together any way so finding 1- or 2-bedrooms home wasn't hard. Now I found yet another way to help them.

I was doing a lot now to help these people and the Community Centers couldn't believe what I had done, and they couldn't do. I was getting these people of the streets and into homes.

This made me feel good inside knowing I was able to help someone else.

There was a lot that needed to be done, but I got things started. I continued to do what I had started because there was a lot of them still out there who needed me.

I found another way I could help these people. I had this 5-acer of land behind me, and I wasn't using. Then I got to thinking about this and knowing where some of these people was living along the Creek banks. So, I had some one come in to look at what I wanted to do to set my place up for tents, I wanted a roof over them and a well put in. I ordered pot a potty for them to use. Then the constructers came in and did the work.

While they were working on this I went out and got some new Tents sleeping bags, blankets and other thing I thought they may need. After the work was done, I started to see who needed a place to live in. I took in 45 people that year.

My list read I'm Feeding and making Sack Lunches, letting them Bath, Washing and Drying their clothes getting them Clothes, having Counselor in by home for Helping them. To help

the Homeless in the Alley Was
and getting them a place to live
in my back field.

I made a list of things I was doing
for them, and after that made
five copies of the list and give
them to five different people.
Then soon after I was getting
help from all over. People was
bringing food clothes, Bath
towel, wash rags, shampoos,
body wash and other things that
was needed. I was getting help,
then I went on the News.

Then somehow, I was getting
money in the mailbox from

people to do what I was doing.
That showed me there was
caring people out there.

There was a lot I can still do with
the help of caring people.

 The Moral of this story is
helping the ones who need you
giving a sack lunch where you
can, help the caring people who
are taking care of the homeless.

Remember this was a DREAM
by Jeannie Lynn.

(Help someone, somewhere, get
something from this dream)

22. The Weekend Sewing Factory

9-29-18

I went to this place with a Friend
and my Quilt that needed fixing.
We came across this lady who
was working there. Then I ask
her if she could work on my
Quilt. She looked at it then said
Yes, leave it here with me. She
was working on someone else
Quilt at that time, so I left mine
there with her. Then she gave
me a ticket with a number on it
and put at one on my Quilt while
I was there.

After that, my friend and I went walking around looking to see who and what else was here on this place. Here were booths setting up making and fixing dolls, toys, shoes. among other things. We came to this Food booth then we stopped for a bit to eat, then we sat at one of their tables to eat. Because we know the Quilt was going to take a while to fix.

The after that we was coming back to where we left my Quilt but

couldn't find the place I left it.it
seems we was lost, we got tuned

around here. We kept on
        walking in hopes we would
        see the lady

where I left my Quilt, but I
        haven't found it yet. I got
        worried and upset

because that was, and old Quilt
from my Grandma and I didn't
want to

lose it. After a while it look like
        everyone was backing up
        for the day

and leaving.

I kept looking for her then my friends wanted us to separate to cover

more ground looking for her. I did find her. I asked her did you get me

quilt done.

She said no but I'll work on it at home and bring it back next weekend.so

I said ok, then she showed me the ticket that she gave me ½ of.

Then she took my Quilt home
with her to fix then she
said she'll be back

next weekend. Now I was out
here looking for my friend
and he was

nowhere to be find.

I started to walk off this place
put still no friend here. It's
seems he left

me there, now I'm alone a no
way home because he
drove me here.

I'm standing here by myself as
I'm walking to the roadside
to go home.

Then this lady with my Quilt
came by and stopped.
Asked where you

going I said home I thought. She
then said get in I'll take
you. she asks

where you are going to
Greenfield. She went on
saying that where I live

to I'll take you so then she took
me home. While she was
driving, we

talked about things and why we were living alone.

Her reasoning was men don't like her cause she a quilter and goes to all

these quilting shows. They don't like these kinds off places. So, I said

that's pretty much me to but men don't want to go with me to these

places either.

I like flea markets and setting up to sale my things. They just don't want to be there with me. But did get home Thanks to her.

The man who took me there stopped by to see if I got home. then I looked at him and said no thanks to you.

The moral of this story doesn't trust the one who took you there the 1st place.

Remember this was a Dream not real. By Jeannie Lynn

23.Some Where I Didn't Know
10/7/18

I was living somewhere in Ky. And I was told to go get lost. I was upset, and I got in my car then started driving. I had no I deal where I was going, I just went.

I couldn't remember how or why I was driving out here, or What happened Why was I out here. I knew I was someone girlfriend put who's, it seems I had lost all senses of who I was.

I didn't have a pocketbook with me, so I could tell anyone who I was. I was still driving with no money to buy gas for the car. Then I ask myself is it my car. I didn't know where I was.

I came to it rest stop and pulled in and stopped there to rest. I stayed there for a full day sleeping. Then someone call the cops then this Lady Cop came knotting on my window of the car. She asks if I was ok or did, I need a doctor. She wanted my Id that I didn't have with me at the time. then she wanted my name and I didn't know that.

 Then she said there a tag on the car I can call that in and find out who you are, so she did that. I had done nothing wrong put got lost she did get my name and find out who I was. She took me in and called these people who cares for lost one until someone claim then.

Then She took me to this house for women who has been where I'm at now. I didn't know anyone there. But they all Welcomed me in the house. They said you will stay here until you can remember who or where you came from. I was not to worry about anything.it been 6 months here.

Then the Lady Cop who found me came to see me, wanted to know are you someone girlfriend a missing reported came in with your picture looking for you. You have a home with him, and you have money. He went and got your car out and took it home and will be back for you. He said you belong with him. That you are getting married soon he thought he had lost you. The Cops question him as to why I was out there driving in the 1st place. Then he told them we had an argument over nothing that mattered at that time.

It was 6months and I didn't think anyone would fine me or claim me. Until this report came in.

I was beginning to be happy where I was and soon, I got to know me for who I was.

Somehow, I knew I was a writer because I told someone I was going to set up and write a story one had come to mine and I wanted to get it down on paper so, this man said lights out soon as you're done.

I didn't know this man at all, so the Lady Cop ask do you want to go with him. I wasn't sure, But I did go with him, he showed me my thing and pictures of us together. Then he showed me the wedding things I had got for our wedding.

Then I began to think well is this my home all my thing are here the clothes here fits me. He then handed me my pocketbook and said look inside and see for yourself.

Then the Lady Cop came to see
me one more time to see if I was
okay.

I told her I'm home Thanks.

Remember It is A Dream not real

24.**Trip to The Food Factory   10-10 18.**

I wanted to take this trip to the Food
Factory and see how they made and
pack the cans. There was this bus
that was picking people up in the
Kroger parking lot. The time of pickup
was 9 am. Everyone needed a ticket
for the ride and there was a lot of us
going. We all got on the bus to go to
the Food Factory. I knowing I have a
Bladder Problem and I wouldn't be
able to hold it for a long trip. The
driver said we will be on the road for
two hours.

Well we are on the bus and it has a
rest room on it which was good. Then
the driver counted all of us and took
our names. so, when we come back,

he would know he has everyone on
the bus. Now we are on our way to
the Food Factory this ride there seem
like this took forever getting there.
The first thing I needed to do was find
the rest room, and it looked like I
wasn't the only one who needed it.

Then the driver who took us here said
I'll be back for you all at 3 pm. To pick
you up. So, everyone meets back
here in this room.

Now we are taking the tour of the
Factory and I saw a lot of things how
the caned the food and seals it. This
tour only took two hours for all of it. I
was lots of rest rooms along the way
we did stop a few times along the
way put my thought was if I got out

of line, they would leave me. So, I held on until the tour was done.

Now it been two hours and the tour are over and we all are looking for the rest room on our way back to the meeting room. We're support to meet the driver to come back home. The drive was coming back at 3pm. to get us.

Well every rest room I came to have someone in them, and I had to go bad. My belly was cramping I didn't know how much longer I could wait. So, I kept walking to the meeting room then I came by anther rest room I stop there and this one was opened so I went in locked the door or, so I thought. Well while on the

pot to pee someone pulled opened
the door and came in. I was setting
there crying because my belly was
hurting, and I couldn't pee to relive
myself.

Then this woman who came in said
I've been there I know how you feel.
Then she said we must hurry it
almost time for the Bus. Then she
turns on the water of the sink and
then I went. She pees in the sink,
then we were both ready to go to the
meeting room for the Bus.

We got to the meeting room and the
Bus was already here, so everyone
was getting on the Bus. Me and this
lady was last getting on, so we sat
together on the Bus. Now we are all

on our way home from the Factory, I'm so glad. The driver did he head count and name calling then found there was one more on the Bus then he has, took here. I told myself I'm not doing this again I was more worried about getting left behind like so many times before from trips I went on.

This Trip I did learn a lot about the Food Factory I did see what I wanted to know and how they caned our foods and pack them. I saw where they stored the foods in the warehouse until they were shipped out to stores. It wasn't clean there we all saw that place.

So YES, do clean the tops of your
can's goods, wipe of the boxes before
opening them. Then wash your hands
good.

 The Moral of this story is anything
you Buy at your market is not Clean,
wash your tops of everything. Can
foods and pop cans.

**Remember these was a Dream   by
Jeannie Lynn.**

#25. God Taking Angles 1=4=2019

I was setting at home and someone
ask are you going to work tomorrow.
It's going to be Hot very Hot. The
news is saying everyone to stay home
in their homes and not go outside.
The heat outside got up to 149
degrees, and if you went out you
want to make it because of the heat.

Then I said I had to go to work my or
be without a job. My employs don't
care about what going on outside.
You be at work or get fired, you don't
have a job.

So, I went to work because it needed
the job to pay my bills, then all of us
went outside to see what was
happing and there were people flying

in the air. There were people flying in the air. It was like Up and away. They were going up hide like God was lifting them and taking them somewhere, people was hanging on to other people.

The cars outside wouldn't run because of the heat it was way too Hot for them. Seeing what was happing outside was a sign that God was taking control of the place and needed all the people to care for others.

I didn't get to finish this dream and don't have the ending for it.

My guess is God is coming and trimming out the flock.

So, beware of the surrounding and watch the heat.

By Jeannie Lynn

Thank You for taking the time reading my book, Jeannie Lynn

26 A dream I'm hoping will come Ture.

This was and still is a planed

 I have wanted to help the homeless people who lives in alley ways, creek banks. This has been something I've wanted for some time now. Put no one wants them in their town but little they know there already there living on their streets. These people have lost their way and have nowhere or no one to go home to. So why are they not allowed to live in a house because they can't afford to.

So, it up to the Caring one to help where we can we can give them clothes blankets and maybe food, then but the people of these towns want let caring people set up a shelter house for them to get them in from the cold and get them help they need. Little talking to them to find out why they are homeless may be the answer.

The town people say they care about you put if you are homeless, *they want nothing to do with you, to the town trash. The homeless* have feeling to, they hurt for someone to love them a hug, and a kind word. Back in 2010 I was going to do something about that but the money we got to do that with got lost the towns people.

As you all know these people was someone parent, did work somewhere, and some still can. You are looking for a housekeeper a babysitter, someone to do yard work. Why not give them a small pay to help you? Some are just looking for a meal or a bath. Talk to them and

see what they need what it going
to hurt you or them.

Find out was some of these
homeless are meet them take
them a sack lunch and
something to drink. This could
be you someday, them people
will walk by who she or he.

This story is not done yet, but I
wanted to share what I had.to
get people thinking. Today as
I'm writing this, I'm planning to
buy some land where on one can
tell me what to do with it, I will
set it up with Campers, and
Storage units made into sleeping

rooms. I will take them form
your town; they will get the help
needed to find out why. We will
get them back on their feet.

Yes, I will need help in getting
this place started, and need beds
another thing in getting up to
start.

If you are one of thought caring
people and want to help and if
you can   **a great help**.

My plan is to Raise a lot of
money with my Sale Books and
Start it Place. Ask for one and I
will get one out to you.

15x15 Units sleeping rooms with toilets and showers and small kitchen net in all them.

15x15 rooms in ea. Unit will be laundry and a gathering room

 12x12 Units sleeping rooms with toilets and showers and small kitchenet

There will be a laundry room and a gathering room. in all units.12x12

  Total of 100 to 200 rooms

Why you ask do I feel so stronger about this, well I was ones homeless and sleeping under bridges and along the creek banks was cold no food no warm bed or clothes to wear, that was the last place I thought I would be. That not a life I want for me or anyone else.

Thank You for reading this Book.
Hope you got something from it. Dreams can and will come true if only you Believe in your Self.

For the Homeless and if you get something from my Dream Go for it, and make it Happen.

You Have My Blessing, Thank you.

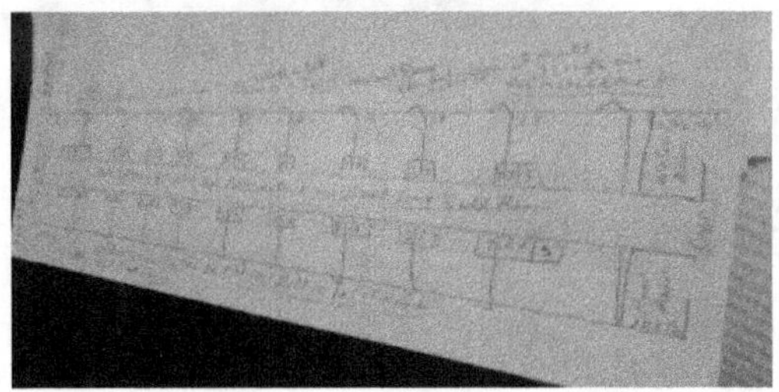

I got married June 22 of 2019.

My dream did come true.

Enjoy the Book. Thanks.

Jeannie Lynn.

{Linda Wilson Atkins}

More Dreams Coming in a new Book